SHERLOCK HOLMES

SILVER BLAZE

SIR ARTHUR CONAN DOYLE

Sweet Cherry

'I'm afraid I shall have to go, Watson,' said Holmes as we were finishing our breakfast one morning.

'Go? Where to?'

'To Dartmoor. To King's Pyland,' he said.

I was surprised that Holmes was not already mixed up in the strange case at King's Pyland. Everyone in the country was talking about it. It was in the newspapers every day.

5

Yet for days, Holmes had done nothing but pace about the room, with his chin on his chest and his brows knitted together in a frown.

Fresh copies of the newspapers were sent to Baker Street every day with reports on the case. But Holmes just glanced at them and then tossed them into a corner.

I could guess what was troubling him.

This must be a problem that could he could not work out.
A famous horse had strangely disappeared. It was the horse who was expected to win the Wessex Cup. And, worse, its trainer had been tragically murdered.

Secretly, I had been hoping that Holmes would take on the case.

'I would be happy to go to King's Pyland with you. As long as I wouldn't be in the way, of course,' I said.

'My dear Watson, I would be very pleased if you would come. I don't think you will be wasting your time. There are parts of this case that will make it unlike any other.'

Holmes reached for his coat. 'I think we have just enough time to catch our train at Paddington. I will explain more on the way. Please bring your best binoculars.'

An hour later, we were sitting in the corner of a first-class carriage, speeding towards Exeter. Sherlock Holmes was flicking through even more newspapers. Finally, he looked up at me.

'Have you read about the murder of John Straker, the trainer? And the disappearance of the racehorse, Silver Blaze?' he asked.

'Yes, of course. I have read the articles in *The Telegraph* and *The Chronicle*,' I answered.

The Daily Telegraph.

25th October 1888

The police are no closer to solving the murder of horse trainer, John Straker. He was killed near King's Pyland Racing Stables on Monday night, 22nd October. The famous racehorse, Silver Blaze, has been missing since the night of the attack. The police have not confirmed whether the two events are connected. They have, however, arrested a man called Fitzroy Simpson, who is being questioned about the crime.

'It is one of those cases when it is more important to think about what we do know than what we don't know,' said Holmes. 'The newspaper reporters are just guessing and inventing stories. We must find out what is true and what is made up.'

He looked me in the eye. He was reminding me that he thought my reports of his cases were too dramatic. Holmes thought I added bits to make the stories more interesting – which is, of course, not true.

'We will gather only the facts,' he went on. 'Then we will see what they tell us. On Tuesday evening, I got a telegram from Colonel Ross. He is the owner of Silver Blaze. I also had one from Inspector Gregory, who is in charge of the case. They both asked for my help.'

'Tuesday evening!' I cried. 'It's Thursday morning now! Why didn't you go there yesterday?'

'Because I made a mistake, my dear Watson. I do make mistakes, though the readers of your stories may not think so. The fact is: I did not think that the most famous horse in England could stay hidden for so long. In the north of Dartmoor of all places! Only a very few people live there.

'Every moment of yesterday I expected to hear that Silver Blaze had been found. I thought that they would find the kidnapper and realise he was also the murderer of John Straker. But nothing happened. Nothing except for the arrest of Fitzroy Simpson. I knew it was time for me to do something.'

'Do you think you know what happened?' I asked.

'I know the main facts of the case. I shall list them for you. It always helps to tell someone. Plus, I can't expect your help if you don't know the facts.'

Holmes explained the events one by one, counting them on his long, thin fingers.

'Silver Blaze is related to a horse called Isonomy. It seems racing must

14

run in the family, as he is just as good a runner as his famous ancestor. Silver Blaze is now in his fifth year of racing. He has won almost every competition out there. Before this disaster, everyone expected him to win the Wessex Cup. Enormous sums of money have been bet on him … and against him. So there are many people who would like to stop Silver Blaze from racing next Tuesday.'

I nodded. I enjoyed a bet, so I understood exactly what Holmes was saying.

'Everyone at the colonel's training stable knows this,' Holmes continued. 'The horse was guarded very carefully. The trainer, John Straker, was a retired jockey. He had worked for Colonel Ross for five years as a jockey and seven as a trainer. He was always an honest man, and was good at his job.

'He had three boys to help him. It is only a small business, with four

16

horses in total. One of the boys sat on guard each night in the stable. The others slept in the loft. All three boys had good, honest characters. John Straker, who was a married man, lived in a small cottage a couple of minutes' walk from the stables. He had no children, kept one servant, and was not short of money.'

Holmes was still marking off the points with his fingers.

'The countryside around there is very quiet,' he went on. 'About half a mile to the north there is a small group of holiday cottages. The town of Tavistock is two miles to the west. And across the moor, about two miles away, is a larger training stables called Capleton. It belongs to Lord Blackwater. The manager there is Mr Silas Brown.

'In every other direction
the countryside is completely
deserted – it's total wilderness.'

I sat, listening carefully.

'On the evening of the crime,
the horses had been exercised and
watered as usual. The stables were
locked up at nine o'clock,' went on

Holmes. 'Two of the boys walked up to the trainer's house. They had supper in the kitchen. The third, Ned Hunter, stayed on guard.

'A few minutes after nine o'clock, a maid called Edith Baxter carried Hunter's supper down to the stables. It was a dish of curried lamb. She carried a lantern with her too, because it was very dark and the path went across the open moor.

'Miss Baxter was almost at the stables when a man appeared out of the darkness. He was dressed

in a gentleman's
clothes: a grey tweed
suit and a cap. He
carried a heavy stick
with a knob on it.
Miss Baxter saw that
his face was very
pale and he seemed
nervous. She guessed
he must be over
thirty years old.

"'Can you tell me
where I am?" the
stranger asked.
"I thought I was

going to have to sleep on the moor. But then I saw the light of your lantern."

"'You are close to the King's Pyland training stables," she said.

"'Oh! What luck!" he cried. "I know that a stable boy eats there alone every night. Is that his supper that you are carrying to him? Hmm … how would you like to earn money for a new dress?" He took out a piece of folded white paper from his waistcoat pocket. "Please give this to the boy tonight. Then you shall have the prettiest dress that money can buy."

'Miss Baxter was frightened by the man. She ran past him to the window of the stables. It was already open. The stable boy, Hunter, was sat at the small table inside. She began to tell him what had just happened. But then the stranger came up behind her.

'"Good evening," the stranger said, looking through the window. "I want to speak to you."

'Miss Baxter said she saw the

piece of folded paper sticking out
of his closed hand.

"'What are you doing here?"
asked Hunter.

"'Giving you the chance to
earn some money," said the man.
"You've got two horses riding in
the Wessex Cup: Silver Blaze and
Bayard. Give me a tip on the race
and I'll pay you. Is it true that
Bayard could beat Silver Blaze?
I've heard that the stable staff
have put their money on him."

"'So you're one of those nasty
touts!" cried Hunter. "I'll show

you how we treat touts in King's Pyland." He sprang up and rushed across the stable to let the dog free. Edith ran away to the house. A minute later, Hunter rushed out with the dog. But the man had vanished.'

'One moment,' I asked. 'When the stable boy ran out with the dog, did he leave the stable door

Touts

These sneaky scoundrels attempt to spy on racehorses and their trainers before a race, to work out who will win. Then they can bet on the horse knowing that they will win the bet and make a lot of money. Touts are obsessed with money and will go to extreme lengths to make sure that they win a bet – even if it means using violence.

unlocked behind him?'

'Excellent, Watson! Excellent!' said Holmes. 'I asked the same question. I sent a telegram to Dartmoor yesterday to find out.'

POST OFFICE
TELEGRAM

No. 16

For free repetition of doubtful words telephone " Telegrams Enquiry " or call, with this form, at office of delivery. Other enquiries should be accompanied by this form and, if possible, the envelope.

Charges to pay
4 s. 4 d
RECEIVED
at Central Telegraph
Office, E.C.1.

Did the stable boy lock the door before chasing the stranger?
Holmes.

Office of Origin and Service Instructions or Nature of Service, if other than telegram.

London, England

Words
12

Received

'They said he did lock the door.
And the window was too small for
a man to climb through.'

I nodded.

'Hunter waited for the other
boys to come back to the stable.
Then he sent a message to John
Straker at the house.

'Straker was worried about
this strange man spying on the
horses. So worried that when Mrs
Straker woke up at one o'clock
in the morning, she found that
her husband was getting dressed.
He said that he couldn't sleep

because he was worried about the horses. He was going down to the stables to check on them. She begged him to stay at home, but he wouldn't.

'Mrs Straker awoke again at seven o'clock in the morning. Her husband was still not back. She dressed quickly and set off for the stables. The door was open. Inside, huddled on a chair, she found Hunter, but she could not wake him up. Silver Blaze's stall was empty. There was no sign of Mr Straker.

'Mrs Straker woke up the two boys who slept in the loft. They had heard nothing during the night. Hunter must have been drugged. They tried and tried, but could not wake him up. He was left to sleep it off while the others ran out to search for Mr Straker and the horse.

At first, they could see no sign of either. They did see something else, though. Something that warned them that a tragedy had occurred.'

Holmes paused and looked at me keenly. I said nothing, but waited for him to continue. 'John Straker's coat was hanging from a bush, flapping in the wind.

Beyond that was a bowl-shaped dip in the moor. At the bottom of the dip was Straker's dead body. He had been hit on the head with a heavy weapon. He also had a long, clean cut on his thigh.

'It was clear that Straker had tried to fight off his attackers. By his body lay a small knife that was covered in blood and a long red and black silk scarf.

The maid, Miss Baxter, said it was the scarf the stranger had been wearing. When Hunter finally woke up he agreed that the scarf belonged to the stranger. He was also sure that the stranger had put sleeping powder into his supper.

'There were hoofprints in the mud, showing that the horse had been there during Mr Straker's murder. But after that, Silver Blaze completely disappeared. A large reward has been offered for anyone who can find him. But, even so, no news has come of him.

'The leftovers of Hunter's supper were tested. It was indeed drugged with sleeping powder. The people at the house ate the same meal, on the same night, without any bad effect. So the powder must have been put in later.'

'And those, Watson, are the main facts of the case. Nothing extra added. I shall now tell you what the police have done.

'Inspector Gregory is in charge of the case. He is a very good officer. If he had a little more imagination, he would be even better. When Inspector Gregory arrived at the stables, he quickly found and arrested the stranger they thought was the criminal. It was not difficult to find him, as he was staying in one of the holiday cottages. His name is Fitzroy

Simpson. He is an educated man, but he wasted his money on horse racing. He now makes money by doing a little quiet bookmaking in London. His betting book shows that he made a bet of five thousand pounds that Silver Blaze would lose the Wessex Cup.

'Simpson said that he had come down to Dartmoor hoping to get information about the King's

Bookmaking

A bookmaker takes bets from gamblers and then pays the money to the winners. If anyone bets on a losing horse, however, the bookmaker keeps the money they have paid him. A clever person could make a lot of money by bookmaking.

Pyland horses. He also wanted
to know about Desborough,
the second favourite horse. He
is trained by Silas Brown at
Capleton Stables.

'Simpson admitted that he had
talked to the maid and stable boy.
But he said he meant no harm.
He just wanted to get information
on the race. When shown his
scarf, Simpson turned very pale.
He did not know how it had got
into Straker's hand. Simpson's
still-wet clothing showed that
he had been out in the storm the

night before. His thick walking stick was weighted with lead. It was just the kind of weapon that could have killed Straker.

'Oddly, though, there were no wounds on Simpson's body. Straker's knife was covered with blood, so he must have stabbed someone. But obviously not Fitzroy Simpson.

37

'There, you have it in a nutshell, Watson. Can you add anything else?'

I had listened with great interest to Holmes' story. I knew most of the facts already. But I had not worked out how they were connected to each other. That is the difference between my mind and Holmes'.

'Is it possible that Straker accidentally cut his own leg? It could have happened in the fight,' I suggested.

'It's more than possible, Watson.

I think it's exactly what happened,' said Holmes.

I was still puzzled. 'So the police think Fitzroy Simpson is guilty?'

'Indeed,' said Holmes. 'The police believe that he drugged the stable lad. Then he kidnapped the horse. Silver Blaze's bridle is missing, so Simpson must have put it on to take him. He was leading the horse away over the hills when he was met by Straker, the trainer. A fight followed. Simpson beat Straker on the head with his heavy stick. Then perhaps the thief led the horse to a secret hiding place. Or it could have run away while Straker and Simpson were fighting. It could still be wandering out on the moors now.

'It's a crazy idea but there doesn't seem to be any other. I shall see if it's the truth when we visit the stables. Until then, we cannot get much further than we are now.'

It was evening before we reached the little town of Tavistock, in the middle of Dartmoor.

With a hiss of steam, the train came to a halt at the small station. We got out of our carriage. Two gentlemen were waiting on the platform. One was a tall, fair man with lion-like hair, a beard and curiously sharp eyes. The other was a small, alert person. He was very neat and dapper, with side whiskers and a monocle.

The tall man was Colonel Ross, the well-known sportsman and owner of Silver Blaze. The other was Inspector Gregory.

'I am pleased that you have come, Mr Holmes,' said the colonel. 'The inspector here has done everything he can. But I do not want to leave any stone unturned.'

'Is there any news?' asked Holmes.

'I am sorry to say that we haven't found many fresh clues,' said the inspector. 'We have a carriage outside. I expect you would like to see King's Pyland before dark. We can talk as we drive.'

A minute later we were all seated in a comfortable carriage. Inspector Gregory and Holmes talked excitedly about the case. But Colonel Ross simply leaned back with his arms folded and his top hat tilted over his eyes.

'The net is drawn pretty close around Fitzroy Simpson,' said Gregory. 'I believe that he is the guilty man.'

'Hmm, are you sure, Inspector?' said Holmes. 'What about Straker's knife?'

'We think that he hurt himself when he fell,' the inspector replied.

'My friend, Dr Watson, said that too. There just doesn't seem to be enough proof to show that Simpson is guilty,' said Holmes.

'I wouldn't say that,' said Gregory. 'He had a reason for wanting the horse to disappear. We think that he drugged the stable boy. He was certainly out in the storm. He was armed with a heavy stick, and his scarf was found in the dead man's hand. I think we have enough to take him to court.'

Holmes shook his head. 'A clever lawyer would tear it all to rags,' he said. 'Why would he take Silver Blaze out of the stable? If he wanted to injure the horse, why didn't he just do it there? Did Simpson have a key to the stable? And which chemist sold him the sleeping powder? Above all, where could he, as a stranger to the area, hide a famous horse? What did he say was on the paper he asked the maid to give to the stable boy?'

'Simpson says the paper was a ten pound

note. One was found in his wallet. I can answer the other questions too. Simpson is not a stranger to the district. He has twice stayed in Tavistock during the summer. The powder was probably brought from London. He could have got a key and then thrown it away after he used it. And the horse may be at the bottom of one of the pits or in the old mines on the moor.'

'What does he say about the scarf?' asked Holmes.

'He says that it is his and that he lost it.'

'Hmm,' Holmes mused. 'There is another training stable quite close, isn't there?'

'Yes, Capleton Stables. Desborough, their horse, was second favourite in the betting. They may have wanted Silver Blaze to disappear so that Desborough could win the race. Silas Brown, Desborough's trainer, is known to have large bets on the race. He was no friend of poor Straker. But we have looked inside their stables and there is nothing to connect him to the case.'

'And nothing to connect Simpson to Capleton Stables?' asked Holmes.

'Nothing at all,' the inspector replied.

Holmes leaned back in his seat. The talk came to an end. A few minutes later our driver pulled up at a neat little red-brick cottage. In the distance was a long grey-tiled outbuilding. In every other direction, the low curves of the moor stretched away to the skyline. Between the hills we could see the steeples of Tavistock and, next to them, a small cluster of houses. I thought that they must be Capleton Stables.

We all sprang out of the carriage, except for Holmes. He still leaned back with his

eyes fixed on the sky in front of him. He was deep in thought. I touched his arm and he jumped, as if he'd been asleep. He stepped out of the carriage.

'Excuse me,' he said, turning to Colonel Ross. 'I was daydreaming.'

There was a glint in his eyes and excitement in his walk. I was sure this meant that he had a clue. Though I could not imagine where he had found it.

'Would you like to go to the scene of the crime, Mr Holmes?' asked Inspector Gregory.

'I think that I would prefer to stay here a little while. I need to check on a few details. I assume that Straker's body was brought back here?'

'Yes, he is lying upstairs. The inquest is tomorrow.'

'He has worked for you for some years hasn't he, Colonel Ross?' asked Holmes.

Inquest

An inquest is made after someone has died, to discover exactly what killed them. A coroner will look at the body and decide how the person died, then discuss it with other doctors and the police. These are often not needed, however – certainly not if I am on the case. I will have likely found the cause of death and the murderer before the inquest is even held.

The colonel nodded. 'He was an excellent worker,' he said.

'I expect you made a list of what Straker had in his pockets, Inspector?'

'I have the things themselves in the sitting room,' said Inspector Gregory. 'Would you like to see them?'

'I would,' Holmes replied.

We all walked into the sitting room and sat around the table. The inspector unlocked a square tin box. He laid a small group of things in front of us, one by one.

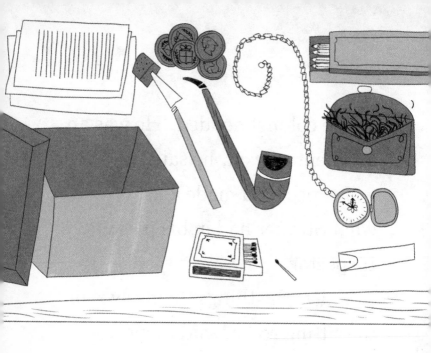

There was a box of matches,
a small candle, a wooden pipe, a
pouch of tobacco, a silver watch
with a gold chain, five gold coins,
a metal pencil case, a few papers,
and a thin knife. The knife had
a very delicate blade. It was
marked Weiss & Co., London.

'This is a very odd knife,' said Holmes. 'It has blood stains on it, so it must be the one that was found in the dead man's hand.'

Holmes handed the knife to me. 'It is a medical knife. Watson, you can probably tell us more about it.'

I took it from him. 'It's what we call a cataract knife.'

'I thought so,' said Holmes. 'A very delicate blade, made for very delicate work. Such as eye operations. It's a strange thing for a man to carry with him. It would not even flip shut to go in his pocket.'

'The tip had a disc of cork on, for safety. We found it beside his body,' said the inspector. 'It was a poor weapon, but perhaps it was the best that he could find at the moment.'

'Very possible,' said Holmes. 'What are these papers?'

'Three of them are receipts from hay dealers,' said the inspector. 'One of them is a letter from Colonel Ross. The other is a dressmaker's bill for

To: *Mr William Derbyshire*

MADAME LESURIER
BOND STREET

thirty-seven pounds and fifteen shillings. It was from Madame Lesurier, of Bond Street. It was meant to go to William Derbyshire. Mrs Straker said that Derbyshire was a friend of her husband. Occasionally his letters are addressed here.'

'Madame Derbyshire has expensive tastes,' said Holmes, looking at the receipt. 'Twenty-two guineas is rather a lot for one dress. But there's nothing more to learn here. Let's go down to the scene of the crime.'

We were just leaving the sitting room when a woman walked towards us. She laid her hand on the inspector's sleeve. Her face was haggard and thin, and overshadowed by sadness.

'Have you got them? Have you found the killer?' she gasped.

'No, Mrs Straker. But Mr Holmes here has come from London to help us. We shall do everything we can,' said the inspector.

'Didn't I meet you in Plymouth, Mrs Straker? At a garden party?' asked Holmes, to my surprise.

'No, sir. You are mistaken.'

'Dear me! Why, I was sure of it. You wore a light grey silk dress with ostrich-feather trimming.'

'I never had such a dress, sir,' answered Mrs Straker.

'I must be mistaken,' he apologised. Then he followed the inspector outside.

I was surprised by Holmes. He is certainly not one for garden parties and would not usually take note of women's dresses, either. I knew then that he was testing a theory. Holmes was obviously well ahead of everyone else. The puzzle was already piecing itself together in his mind.

We walked across the hills to the hollow where the body was found. At the edge of it was the bush where the coat had hung.

'There was no wind that night, I understand,' said Holmes.

'No wind, but very heavy rain,' replied the inspector.

'So the overcoat was not blown against the bush. It was put there.'

'Yes, it was laid across the bush,' the inspector agreed.

'The ground has been trampled on a lot. No doubt many feet have been here since Monday night,' said Holmes.

'No. A piece of matting was laid at the side. We all stood on that,' said Inspector Gregory.

'Excellent,' said Holmes.

Gregory handed him a bag.

'In here is one of the boots that Straker wore. I also have one of Fitzroy Simpson's shoes. Plus, there's a cast horseshoe of Silver Blaze.'

'My dear inspector, you outdo yourself!' Holmes took the bag and we followed him into the muddy hollow. He kneeled down on the matting and carefully studied the trampled mud in front of him.

'What's this?' he said, suddenly. He picked up something very small and held it up for us to see. It was a half-burned match, covered in mud.

'I cannot think how I missed it,' said Inspector Gregory. He looked annoyed.

'It was buried in the mud. I only saw it because I was looking for it,' said Holmes.

'What! You expected to find it?' asked the inspector.

'Yes.'

Holmes took the shoes from the bag and matched each to the footprints on the ground. Then he climbed up to the edge of the hollow and crawled about in the bushes. We followed him.

'There are no more tracks,' said Inspector Gregory. 'I have studied the ground very carefully.'

Holmes got up and brushed his trousers. 'I would not have the cheek to do it again then. But I'd like to take a walk over the moor before it gets dark. I think that I

shall put this horseshoe
in my pocket for luck.'

I looked at Holmes sharply.
He was up to something again.
A horseshoe for luck! He didn't
believe in such things.

Colonel Ross was pacing up
and down and frowning. He
was certainly an impatient man.
He did not like Holmes' quiet
and careful way of working. He
looked at his watch.

'Will you come back with me,
Inspector?' he asked, turning to
Gregory. 'I would like your advice

on some things. I wonder whether it would be best to remove Silver Blaze's name from the entries for the race.'

'Certainly not!' cried Holmes. 'Let the name stay.'

The colonel bowed. 'Thank you for the advice, sir,' he said, sharply. 'You will find us at poor Straker's house when you have finished your walk. We can drive together into Tavistock.'

The colonel took the inspector back to the house. Holmes and I walked slowly across the moor.

The sun was beginning to sink behind the stables of Capleton. The green hills were tinged with gold and brown, as the ferns and brambles caught the evening light. But Holmes missed the beauty of the landscape because he was deep in thought.

'Watson,' he said at last. 'Let's leave the mystery of who killed John Straker for a moment. We should concentrate on finding the lost horse.'

I agreed.

'Silver Blaze escaped during or after Straker's murder. Where could he have gone? Horses like to be with other horses. I think he would either return to his stable or go over to Capleton Stables, where there are other horses. If he was running wild across the hills he would have been seen by now.

If anyone found him, they could not sell him. He is too famous.'

I nodded. 'But where is he, then?'

'Well, he's not at King's Pyland. So, surely, he must be at Capleton Stables. This part of the moor is very hard and dry. It slopes away towards Capleton. There is a long hollow over there. It would have been very wet on Monday night. So if the horse went to Capleton Stables, we will see his tracks in that hollow.'

We had been walking quickly as we talked. In a few minutes we reached the hollow. Holmes asked me to walk down to the right, and he went to the left. I had not taken fifty steps before I heard him shout and saw him waving to me.

When I reached his side I saw horse tracks in the mud. Holmes took the horseshoe from his pocket and placed it in a hoofprint. It fitted exactly! I knew he wasn't keeping the horseshoe for luck.

'You see how important it is to have imagination?' said Holmes. 'It is the one thing that Inspector Gregory doesn't have.

We imagined what might have happened. Then we acted on it, and we were correct! Let's go.'

We lost the tracks from time to time, but then found more closer to Capleton. It was Holmes who saw them first. He stood pointing at them. There were a man's footprints next to the horse tracks.

'But the horse was alone before!' I cried.

'Yes. It *was* alone before,' said Holmes, with his eyes still glued to the ground. 'What's this?'

The tracks turned sharply off towards King's Pyland. Holmes whistled and we both followed the trail. His eyes were carefully inspecting the tracks. But I looked to the side and saw the same tracks coming back in the opposite direction.

'Look, Holmes!' I said in surprise.

'Excellent spot, Watson!' said Holmes, when I pointed it out. 'You have saved us a long walk, which would have just taken us back in a circle. Let's follow the return track.'

We didn't have far to walk. The prints ended at the path that led up to the gates of Capleton Stables. As we got nearer, a man ran out.

'We don't want any strangers around here,' he said.

'I just want to ask a question,' said Holmes. He stood with his finger and thumb in his waistcoat pocket. 'Could I see Mr Silas Brown if I came back at five o'clock tomorrow morning?'

The man relaxed. 'Well, here he is now, sir. He can answer your question himself.'

As Holmes was about to give him a tip, the man said, 'No, sir, no. I will lose my job if he sees me taking your money. Afterwards, if you like.'

Holmes put the coin back into his pocket. A fierce-looking old man came out of the gate. He was swinging a hunting crop in his hand.

'What's this, Dawson!' he cried. 'No chatting! Get on with your work! And you, what do you want here?'

'To talk with you for a few

minutes, my good sir,' said
Holmes, in the sweetest of voices.

'I haven't got time to talk
to anyone. We don't want any
strangers here. Be off, or I'll let
the dog chase you.'

Holmes leaned forwards and
whispered something in the
trainer's ear. The old man jumped
and his face glowed bright red.

'It's a lie!' he shouted.

'A terrible lie!'

'Shall we argue about it in public?' asked Holmes. 'Or talk it over in your office?'

'Oh, come in if you must,' the man said.

Holmes smiled. 'I shall not keep you more than a few minutes,' he said.

Twenty minutes later, Holmes and the trainer finally came out of the office. Never had I seen anyone change so much in such a short time. Silas Brown's face was very pale and I could see drops of sweat on his forehead.

His hands shook, making his hunting crop wobble like a branch in the wind. His bullying bossiness was all gone. He squirmed at Holmes' side like a scared puppy.

'I will do what you've asked,' he said.

'There must be no mistake,' said Holmes, looking round at him. The man winced as he heard the seriousness in Holmes' voice.

'Oh, no, there shall be no mistake. It will be there. Shall I change it first or not?'

Holmes thought for a moment and then burst out laughing. 'No, don't,' he said. 'I shall write to you about it. No tricks now, or …'

'Oh, you can trust me, you can trust me!'

'Yes, I think I can. Well, you will hear from me tomorrow.' Holmes turned, ignoring the hand the man held out to him. We set off for King's Pyland.

'I have never met a man quite like Silas Brown. He is a bully, a coward and a sneak,' said Holmes as we walked along together.

'He has the horse, then?' I asked.

'Yes. He tried to lie. But when I told him exactly what he had done that morning, he thought that I had been watching him. You must have noticed the square toes in the footprints, Watson? His boots matched them exactly.'

I had not noticed that, but I was not going to admit it.

'I described to him how he was the first down to the stables, when he saw a strange horse wandering over the moor. I told him how he went out to it, and recognised it by the white patch on its forehead. It was Silver Blaze. This was his chance to take Silver Blaze out of the competition, so that his horse, Desborough, could win. That way, he'd win all his bets.'

It was all becoming clear to me.

'I told Silas Brown that he first planned to take the horse straight back to King's Pyland,' Holmes went on. 'But then an evil thought had come to him. He could hide the horse until the race was over. So he led Silver Blaze back to Capleton, and hid him in the stables. When I told him every detail, he gave up trying to lie.'

'But his stables were searched,' I said.

'An old horse dealer like him has many tricks,' said Holmes.

'But aren't you afraid to leave Silver Blaze with him? He might hurt him.'

'My dear Watson, he will guard the horse with his life. He knows that if he keeps the horse safe, he might get less of a punishment.'

'Colonel Ross does not seem like someone who would show mercy to the man who took his horse,' I said.

'This is not only Colonel Ross' decision. I will decide what I do or don't tell the police. That is the good thing about being a private detective. I don't know whether you saw it, Watson, but the colonel has been a little rude to me. I feel like playing a little joke on him now. Don't say anything about the horse.'

'Certainly not.'

'And, of course, we have only answered the small mystery. We still need to find out who killed John Straker.'

'And will you look into that now?' I asked.

'Certainly not. We will both go back to London by the night train,' replied Holmes.

I was shocked at my friend's words. We had only been in Devonshire for a few hours. I couldn't understand why he would give up a case that was going so well. He wouldn't say another word until we were back at Straker's house. The colonel and the inspector were waiting for us in the sitting room.

'Watson and I shall return to London by the midnight train,' said Holmes. 'We have had a charming little breath of your beautiful Dartmoor air.'

The inspector opened his eyes
wide in surprise. The colonel's lip
curled into a sneer.

'So you are giving up! You will
not find the murderer of
poor John Straker?'
asked the colonel.

Holmes shrugged. 'There are lots of difficulties in the way,' he said. 'But I am sure that your horse will run on Tuesday. Please have your jockey ready. May I have a photograph of Mr John Straker?'

The inspector took one from an envelope and handed it to

Holmes.

'My dear Inspector Gregory, you think of everything.

Can you wait here for a moment? I have a question that I would like to ask the maid.'

'I'm rather disappointed in our London consultant,' said Colonel Ross, as Holmes left the room. 'He hasn't helped at all.'

'At least you have his word that your horse will run,' I said.

'Yes,' said the colonel, shrugging. 'But I would prefer to have the horse.'

I was about to reply, defending Holmes, when he came back into the room again.

'Now, gentlemen,' he said. 'I am ready to go back to Tavistock Station.'

One of the stable boys held the carriage door open for us. As we stepped in, a thought popped into Holmes' mind. He touched the boy on his sleeve.

'Who looks after the sheep in the paddock?' he asked.

'I do, sir.'

'Has there been anything wrong with them lately?'

'Well, no, not much, sir. But three of them have gone lame,

sir. They seem to have hurt their legs.'

Holmes seemed very pleased. He chuckled and rubbed his hands together.

'A big guess, Watson,' he said, pinching my arm. 'Gregory, did you hear about the strange thing that has happened to the sheep?'

Colonel Ross still looked disappointed that Holmes seemed so useless. But the inspector looked curious.

'You think it's important?' he asked.

'Very important,' replied Holmes.

'Is there any particular point that I should note?'

'The curious incident of the dog in the night-time.'

'The dog did nothing in the night-time.'

'That was the curious incident,' said Holmes. 'Drive on, coachman!'

That gave me something to think about for the rest of the journey.

For the next few days I didn't see much of Holmes. Then, on Tuesday, we caught the train to

Winchester. We were going to see the Wessex Cup horse race. Colonel Ross met us outside the station. We drove in his private coach to the racecourse outside the town. His face was serious.

'I have not seen my horse,' he said.

'Would you recognise him when you saw him?' asked Holmes.

The colonel grew very angry. 'I have been in horse racing for twenty years, and no one has asked me that before,' he said.

'A child would know
Silver Blaze,
with his white
forehead.'
'How is the betting?'
Holmes asked.

'Well, that's the strange part of
it,' said the colonel, changing his
tone. 'The betting odds have got
shorter and shorter. Yesterday,
it seemed no one thought Silver
Blaze would win. But today,
everyone believes he will.'

'Hmm,' said Holmes. 'Somebody
knows something, that is clear.'

As we arrived at the racecourse, I glanced at the list of horses who would be running.

THE WESSEX CUP

Mr Heath Newton's Midnight Runner.
Red cap. Brown jacket.
Colonel Wardlaw's Pugilist.
Pink cap. Blue and black jacket.
Lord Backwater's Desborough.
Yellow cap and sleeves.
Colonel Ross' Silver Blaze.
Black cap. Red jacket.
Duke of Balmoral's Iris.
Yellow and black-striped
cap and sleeves.
Lord Singleford's Rasper.
Purple cap. Black sleeves.

'Look!' I cried. 'All six horses are there!'

'All six there? Then my horse is running,' cried the colonel. 'But I don't see him.'

'Only five have passed us. This must be him now,' I said.

As I spoke, a large horse came out of the weighing room and cantered past us. On its back was

a jockey wearing a black and red silk outfit – the colours of the colonel.

'That's not my horse!' cried Colonel Ross. 'He doesn't have a white hair on his head. What have you done, Mr Holmes?'

'Well, let us see how he gets on,' said my friend, calmly. Holmes peered through my binoculars at the horses, just as the race began. 'An excellent start!' he said. 'There they are, coming around the bend!'

The six horses were so close together that a rug could have covered them. But halfway up the straight side of the track, the Capleton horse, Desborough, moved into the lead. Before they reached us, however, he slowed down and Silver Blaze gave a

spurt of speed. Silver
Blaze passed the winning
post seconds before his
rival.

'We've won!' gasped
the colonel. He put his
hands over his eyes.

'I have no idea how we've won, but we did. Can you tell me the truth, Mr Holmes? What's going on?'

'Certainly, Colonel. You shall know everything. Let's all go and see Silver Blaze.'

We made our way into the weighing enclosure, where the owners and friends could see the horses.

The colonel stared at the winning horse, looking confused. Holmes waved at a stable boy who gave him a bucket of water

and a sponge. He rubbed the
horse's forehead. Amazingly, the
white patch began to show.

'There you see,' said Holmes.
'The same old Silver Blaze as ever.'

'I cannot believe it,' said
Colonel Ross.

'I found him in the hands of a dealer,' explained Holmes. 'He had given him this clever disguise to hide his identity. I thought that we should let him race in it.'

'My dear sir, you have worked wonders.' The colonel had changed from confused to delighted in a single second. 'I owe you a thousand apologies for saying you had not helped in the case. You have helped hugely. Thank you for getting my horse back. I would thank you even more if you could find John Straker's murderer.'

'I have done that too,' said Holmes, quietly.

The colonel and I stared at him. We were amazed.

'You have got him! Where is he, then?' asked the colonel.

'He's here,' replied Holmes.

'Here! Where?' cried the colonel.

'Right here, with us, right now.'

The colonel's face turned red. 'I am thankful for you finding my horse, Mr Holmes. But what you have just said is either a very bad joke or an insult!' he shouted.

Holmes laughed.

'I am not saying you are the murderer, Colonel. The real murderer is standing right behind you.' Holmes placed his hand on the glossy neck of Silver Blaze.

'The horse!' the colonel and I cried.

'Yes, the horse. But it was done in self-defence. You should not have trusted John Straker. But there goes the bell, and I could win a little money on this next race.

We shall continue this talk later.'

I had placed one or two bets too, and even won a few of them. Holmes and I were both in happy moods during the train ride back to London.

The journey went quickly as Colonel Ross and I listened to Holmes' story.

'All the theories I had made from reading the newspaper reports were completely wrong,' he said. 'There were some important clues in them, but they were hidden by other details. When we first went to Dartmoor, I was sure that Fitzroy Simpson was the murderer. But it was while we were in the carriage, heading to Straker's, that a clue came to me. The stable boy's curry!

'You remember that I was deep in thought? I stayed sitting in the carriage after you had all got out. It was because I was so surprised that I missed such an obvious clue.'

'I cannot see how the curry is a clue,' said the colonel. But I was beginning to see what Holmes was getting at.

'It was the first link in my chain of deduction,' Holmes continued.

'Sleeping powder doesn't taste bad, but you can notice the taste. If it were mixed with an ordinary meal the stable boy would have tasted the poison and left the rest of his dinner. A spicy curry was exactly the thing to hide its taste.

'There is no way that Fitzroy Simpson could have planned for Straker's family to eat curry that night – he didn't live with them, or even speak to them. Therefore, Simpson was not a suspect in the case. Then I looked at Straker and his wife. They were the only two people who could have chosen curried lamb for supper that night. No one else who ate the curry was drugged. So the sleeping powder was obviously added after the dish was put aside for the stable boy. Which of them, then, could have put something in that dish without the maid seeing them?

'I hadn't worked out the answer to that question, but I had worked out the importance of the silent dog. When the stable boy met Simpson, he threatened to let the stable dog loose. So how had someone got in at midnight and stolen Silver Blaze without the dog barking and waking up the other boys? It had to be someone the dog knew well.

'I was almost sure that it was Straker who

went down to the stables in the middle of the night and took out Silver Blaze. But why? It had to be a dishonest reason. Why would he drug his own stable boy if not?

'I've heard of some trainers earning a lot of money by betting against their own horses. They make sure their horse loses, so they win the money. Sometimes they even offer money to the jockey to lose on purpose. And sometimes they think of an even cleverer way to do it. What was it here? I thought that seeing what was in his pockets might help me work out the answer.

'And it did. Do you remember the strange knife that was found in the dead man's hand? Watson, you told us that it is used for the most delicate surgical operations. It was going to be used for a delicate operation that night.

'You will know, Colonel Ross, that even the tiniest cut in the horse's back leg will stop it from running properly. You would not see the cut easily. And you would think that it was a muscle strain or swelling of some sort. No one would think that the trainer was committing a crime.'

'Villain!' cried the colonel.

'This is why John Straker took Silver Blaze out onto the moor. He was going to cut the horse's leg to stop him from running. But Silver Blaze is a very excitable animal. If Straker cut him in the stable, he would have neighed and woken up the other boys. He had to do it outside, where he couldn't be heard.'

'I have been blind!' cried the colonel. 'And that was why you found the muddy match! He was trying to light his candle, to see what he was doing.'

'Yes. And when I looked in his belongings, I found more. I discovered both how and why he did the crime. You see, most men do not carry other people's bills about in their pockets. We have enough bills of our own to pay! So at once I knew that Straker was leading a double life and that the bill was his.

'The bill showed us that he was buying expensive dresses for a lady. I know you pay your staff well, Colonel, but I still don't think they would have enough money to buy twenty-guinea dresses. I asked Mrs Straker about the dress – pretending that I had seen her in it at a garden party – but she said it wasn't hers. So I wrote down the dressmaker's address and took the photograph of Straker to show her when I visited.

MADAME LESURIER
BOND STREET

TO: *Mr William Derbyshire*

113

'From that time on, the whole mystery started to clear up. Straker had led the horse out to the hollow so no one could see or hear him. As Fitzroy Simpson ran away from the stable, he dropped his scarf. Straker picked it up. Maybe he thought he could hold the horse's leg with it.

'When Straker was in the hollow, he got behind the horse and struck a match to light his candle. But that scared Silver Blaze. He lashed out and kicked Straker on the head. That's why

we thought Straker has been hit
by something heavy and made
of metal – it was a horseshoe.
Straker had already taken off
his overcoat and
hung it on the
bush. And
the cut on

his thigh was just an accident that happened when he fell to the floor, after Silver Blaze killed him.'

'Wonderful!' cried the colonel. 'Wonderful! It's as if you were there.'

'My final idea was a big guess. I thought that a clever man like Straker would not do the delicate operation on the horse without practising. I wondered what would he practise on? Then I saw the sheep. I asked the stable boy about them and his answer showed me that I was correct.

116

Straker had injured some of the sheep by practising the operation on them.

'When I got back to London I visited the dressmaker. She looked at the picture of Straker and said it was a customer of hers: Mr Derbyshire. His wife liked expensive dresses. This second wife must have cost Straker all his money. That is what led him to make this evil plan. If he bet on the second favourite horse, Desborough, the odds would be much better, meaning that he would win more money. Straker could then make sure Silver Blaze was injured, so he couldn't race.'

'You have explained all but one thing,' said the colonel. 'Where was the horse?'

'It ran away and was cared for by one of your neighbours at Capleton Stables. You must thank him.' Holmes looked out the window. 'This is Clapham Junction. We shall be at Victoria Station in less than ten minutes. Would you like to come to our rooms for a drink,

Colonel? I can tell you more
details on the case, if you'd like?'

The colonel smiled and nodded.

I sat back into my seat to have
a good think about Holmes' story.
It all seemed so simple that I
wondered why I had not worked
it out myself. It's probably why I
am a doctor and he is a detective.

Sherlock Holmes

World-renowned private detective Sherlock Holmes has solved hundreds of mysteries, and is the author of such fascinating monographs as *Early English Charters* and *The Influence of a Trade Upon the Form of a Hand.* He keeps bees in his free time.

Dr John Watson

Wounded in action at Maiwand, Dr John Watson left the army and moved into 221B Baker Street. There he was surprised to learn that his new friend, Sherlock Holmes, faced daily peril solving crimes, and began documenting his investigations. Dr Watson also runs a doctor's practice.

To download Sherlock Holmes activities, please visit www.sweetcherrypublishing.com/resources